For my mother, who helped me achieve getting published

Published in the United States
by Xist Publishing
www.xistpublishing.com
24200 Southwest Freeway
Suite 402- 290
Rosenberg, TX 77471

Hardcover ISBN: 978-1-5324-1602-6
Paperback ISBN: 978-1-5324-1601-9
eISBN: 978-1-5324-1600-2

Printed in the USA

Squirrel & Bear
Take to the Air

Patrick Brooks

Squirrel wanted to fly.

"Get your head out of the clouds!" his family said.

The birds chased him away.

But Squirrel found Bear.

BEAR'S HOUSE

It was time to make a plan.

Was a catapult the solution?

Or a squirrel -copter?

Or an airship?

Those mean
birds!

Owl had an idea.

They flew across the sea.

A plan was constructed.

And Squirrel and his new friends flew higher than the birds.

CPSIA information can be obtained
at www.ICGtesting.com
Printed in the USA
BVHW020925111021
618670BV00005B/118